Dreams Come True

Danielle Star

Scholastic Inc.

The publisher does not have any control over and does not assume any responsibility for author or third-party websites or their content.

All names, characters, and related indicia contained in this book are the copyright and exclusive license of Atlantyca S.p.A. in their original version. The translated and/or adapted versions are the property of Atlantyca S.p.A. All rights reserved.

Published by Scholastic Inc., *Publishers since 1920*, 557 Broadway, New York, NY 10012. SCHOLASTIC and associated logos are trademarks and/or registered trademarks of Scholastic Inc.

This book is a work of fiction. Names, characters, places, and incidents are either the product of the author's imagination or are used fictitiously, and any resemblance to actual persons, living or dead, business establishments, events, or locales is entirely coincidental.

ISBN 978-1-338-15174-9

Text by Danielle Star
Original title *Il sogno si avvera*

Editorial cooperation by Lucia Vaccarino
Illustrations by Emilio Urbano (layout),
Nicoletta Baldari (clean up), and Patrizia Zangrilli (color)
Graphics by Danielle Stern

Special thanks to Tiffany Colón
Translated by Chris Turner
Interior design by Baily Crawford

10 9 8 7 6 5 4 3 2 1   18 19 20 21 22

Printed in the U.S.A.   40
First printing 2018

Contents

Imagine a magical land wrapped in golden light. A planet in a distant galaxy beyond the known stars. This enchanted place is known as Aura, and it is very special. For Aura is home to the pegasus, a winged horse with a colorful mane and coat.

The pegasuses of Aura come from four ancient island realms that lie within Aura's enchanted oceans: the Winter Realm of Amethyst Island, the Spring Realm of Emerald Island, the Day Realm of Ruby Island, and the Night Realm of Sapphire Island.

A selected number from each realm are born with a symbol on their wings and a hidden magical power. These are the Melowies.

When their magic beckons them in a dream, all Melowies leave their island homes to answer the call. They must attend school at the Castle of Destiny, a legendary castle hidden in a sea of clouds, where they will learn all about their hidden powers. Destiny is a place where friendships are born, where Melowies find their courage, and where they discover the true magic inside themselves!

Map of Aura

The Day Realm

Castle of Destiny

The Night Realm

Map of the Castle of Destiny

1 Butterfly Tower—first-year dormitory

2 Dragonfly Tower—second-year dormitory

3 Swallow Tower—third-year dormitory

4 Eagle Tower—fourth-year dormitory

5 Principal Gia's office

6 Library

7 Classrooms

8 The Winter Tower

9 The Spring Tower

10 The Day Tower

11 The Night Tower

12 Waterfall

13 Runway

14 Assembly hall

15 Garden

16 Sports fields

17 Cafeteria

18 Kitchen

19 Auditorium

Meet the Melowies

Cleo

Her realm: unknown
Her personality:
impulsive and loyal
Her passion: writing
Her gift: something
mysterious . . .

Electra

Her realm: Day
Her personality: boisterous
and bubbly
Her passion: fashion
Her gift: the Power of
Light

Maya

Her realm: Spring
Her personality: shy and sweet
Her passion: cooking
Her gift: the Power of Heat

Cora

Her realm: Winter
Her personality: proud and sincere
Her passion: ice-skating
Her gift: the Power of Cold

Selena

Her realm: Night
Her personality: deep and sensitive
Her passion: music
Her gift: the Power of Darkness

1
The Big Day

Something very special was happening. Way up in the sky above the land of Aura, a magical trail had appeared in the clouds. It would only remain there for one day. Twenty-four pairs of wings fluttered in the cool air. Twenty-four silky manes sparkled in the morning light. Today was the big day. The day the Melowies were going to the Castle of Destiny for the first time!

Maya flapped her pink wings. She'd left

her home in the Spring Realm and was now flying with a bunch of other special pegasuses to the place they'd all dreamed about since they were little. She was so excited to finally find out more about her magic! It was just a shame that she was too shy to share her excitement with the others. But maybe, with a little effort . . .

Maya spotted a group of girls giggling nearby. She took a deep breath, flew over to them, and summoned her courage. "Hi, girls! How are you?" she whispered. The words were so soft that the others didn't hear. They glided away on a whistling air current without even noticing her.

Feeling disappointed, Maya watched them flying off into the distance. But then she noticed a pegasus with a purple mane who was floating all by herself. Maya flew over to her with a flutter of wings. "HELLO! WHAT'S YOUR NAME?" she said, this time far too loudly.

The stranger looked her up and down. In a flat voice, she answered, "Selena."

"I'm Maya. Umm . . . are you a Melowy, too?" Maya asked, trying to make conversation.

"Of course," the pretty pegasus replied.

Now Maya felt silly. Selena had to be a Melowy! Only Melowies, the pegasuses born with a symbol on their wings and a hidden magical power, could go where they were going.

Selena gave her a sideways look. Did Maya

know how important this journey was? Selena wasn't trying to be nasty. But she usually liked to be alone and wanted to enjoy the special moment without distractions. Besides, Selena wasn't used to being around other Melowies. At home, in her mother's castle, she was the only one she'd ever known.

Suddenly, an "Ooh!" echoed along the path through the clouds. The Melowy who had been flying at the front of the herd, Cora from the Winter Realm, suddenly seemed to lose her perfect poise. Her blue eyes grew wide with wonder as she gazed at what lay ahead.

The Melowies saw an island floating in the middle of a sea of clouds! The island was crowned by a beautiful castle with soaring towers surrounded by homes and other buildings below. It was the Castle of Destiny, the school for Melowies. And it was just as Cora had always imagined it! She'd been waiting to come here since she was a tiny pegasus, and finally, her time had come. She wanted everything to be perfect.

"Wings out, chin up, look proud," she said to herself as she recovered her composure and followed the last stretch of the sparkling path through the clouds. She took a deep breath. "Wings out, chin—"

"*Coming through!*" someone suddenly yelled from behind her. And before Cora

could get out of the way, a Melowy with a fiery red mane flew right into her, knocking her—and all her perfect plans—upside down!

Meanwhile, on the floating island of Destiny, a little pegasus named Cleo peered out the window at the crowded streets and sighed.

"Cleo! Sweetheart!" called Theodora, the school cook. She held a cupcake covered with candles for Cleo's arrival day. Ever since Gia, the school principal, found baby Cleo on the front steps of the castle, Cleo had celebrated that day with a sticky-sweet cupcake from the cook.

"Make a wish and blow out the candles!" said Theodora, while Fluffy, Cleo's adorable puppy, danced between her legs, hoping for a taste. As usual, Theodora had dressed Fluffy—she was covered from head to paw with little pink bows.

Cleo snorted. *Make a wish! As if anything could be that simple today!*

Theodora adjusted a runaway lock of Cleo's hair. "What's the matter, honey bun? Don't you like the cupcake I made you? It's double chocolate with three kinds of sprinkles, just the way you like."

"I'm sorry, Theodora,"

mumbled Cleo. "The cupcake is wonderful. It's just that . . . No, it's nothing. I'm a little distracted today, that's all."

The cook giggled. "You're always a little distracted! Remember when you were little and went to play on the airfield during landing practice? Or the time you accidentally shut yourself in the cupboard of forbidden magic? But we like you just as you are. Now I've got to run! They need me in the kitchen. You finish that breakfast, young lady!" Theodora planted a big kiss on Cleo's forehead.

"Okay," said the little pegasus, trying to smile. "See you at the party tonight."

Cleo had always loved her arrival day because it fell on the day that new students arrived at the Castle of Destiny. But this year everything was different. This year she was the same age as the new students. And no matter how hard she wished, she could never be one of them. Unlike the other Melowies,

she didn't have a symbol on her wings. She was the only one who didn't know which realm she comes from. And that was all she could think about when she blew out the candles.

Cleo didn't know that sometimes impossible dreams *can* come true. And in the most unexpected ways . . .

2

The First Day of the Rest of Their Lives

Cleo felt a little better after she finished her arrival day cupcake. She decided not to let bad thoughts ruin her special day. *I'll enjoy the welcome ceremony, like I do every year,* she thought.

Cleo looked up into the sky and admired the new students gliding gracefully toward the front yard of the school. Together, they looked like one big, rainbow cloud. She had to get a better view! So Cleo spread her wings and flew as fast as she could toward the top of the castle.

From up among the clouds, the Castle of Destiny looked more beautiful than ever.

"No," Cleo said to herself. "I can't possibly be sad today."

"Wow! I'm finally at the Castle of Destiny!" cried the Melowy with the fiery red mane.

Cora fixed her long ponytail and glared at the bubbly Melowy behind her.

The girl ignored Cora's icy look and introduced herself.

"Hi, I'm Electra, from the Day Realm.   What's your name?"

"Cora. Winter Realm."

"Oh, that explains why you gave me that cold look!" Electra answered, giggling.

Cora gave her another frosty glare.

"Sorry! I chose the wrong words," Electra explained. "But I really wasn't making fun of you! I was just trying to break the ice!"

Cora shrugged. "Look, that's Principal Gia over there. She's about to give the welcome speech."

The principal rang a golden bell. Rays of bright light sprang out in every direction as it chimed. The Melowies looked on in awe.

"Welcome to the Castle of Destiny," said Gia. "Although it's been many years since I was a student, and my mane is now almost

completely silver, I still remember the excitement of my very first day at this school. Like me, you will learn to use your power and discover your place in the world of Aura. Please look around and soak in as much of this day as you can—the faces, the smells, the feelings, everything. In the future you will remember this moment as the first day of the rest of your lives!"

"How thrilling!" beamed Electra. "But first we have to pass the entrance test," she added. Electra tried to look brave, but inside, her tummy was doing somersaults.

Selena stared nervously down at her hooves. Her mother was the queen of the Night Realm and expected Selena to follow in her hoofprints. She was scared to learn more about her powers and her future. What if her fate was not the future her mother expected of her?

Maya started backing away and closed her wings tightly around her body, the way she always did when she was nervous. Not looking where she was going, she accidentally stepped on Cora's tail.

"Be careful!" Cora shrieked. "You'll mess up my hairdo!" She wanted to look perfect on the first day of this journey! A journey that would lead her to the throne of the Winter Realm. She was sure of it!

"Wh-what if I fail the test?"

asked Maya with a bit of a stammer. "B-before I came here, everything seemed possible. Now I know I'll never make it . . ."

"Don't count yourself out!" snapped Cora. "We don't even know what kind of test it is yet!"

Maya blushed and went quiet, her wings wrapping around herself even tighter.

Riiiiip!

The sound of tearing cloth caught all the Melowies off guard. Then suddenly a flag hanging from the top of the castle came falling down. Tangled up inside was a young pegasus with a rosy mane.

"Who is that?" Cora wondered.

3
An Unexpected Meeting

The Melowies laughed as Cleo untangled herself from the flag and flew back up to the castle tower as quickly as she could.

Maya sighed and shook her head. She wanted to tell the Melowies who were laughing to be quiet, but she was too shy. *Maybe Cora will give them one of her icy glares*, she thought. *Maybe behind that snooty exterior, Cora's not that bad.*

But it was Principal Gia's voice that rang out. "Follow me," she announced, then walked into the castle as though nothing had happened.

The Melowies trotted after her with a mixture of curiosity and wonder. Their home realms were all beautiful in their own way. But the Castle of Destiny was different. It was more bewitching and majestic than any place they had ever seen before.

Principal Gia took them on a quick tour of the school. She led them through rooms filled with globes, beautiful paintings, maps, and mysterious instruments. She walked quickly, and the Melowies scurried to keep up with her. "Hurry," Principal Gia said, "you'll have time to take a closer look at everything after the entrance exam."

But the Melowies couldn't help peeking into every room. They were enchanted by

the incredible stained glass windows that reached the ceiling and filled the whole school with colored light.

For a moment, Maya forgot to be afraid and stopped to look up at one of the stained

glass windows. It showed a pegasus soaring through a pink sky.

"Isn't it beautiful?" she asked. The room was silent—everyone had gone! "No," she moaned. "I'm lost! I'm so silly!"

Maya ran around the next bend in the corridor, but there was no trace of the rest of the group. Worse than that, there were three different paths in front of her and she didn't know which one to take.

A pegasus with a rosy mane poked her head out from behind a door.

"Hey! You're the one who . . .," Maya began but stopped herself. It wouldn't be nice to say, "You're the one who just made a fool of herself in front of everyone."

"Who got all twisted up in the flag like a

pretzel?" the pegasus with the rosy mane said without a hint of embarrassment. "My name's Cleo. After I untangled myself, I flew back here. And when I heard Gia and the other Melowies coming, I hid. I never

expected to find a straggler!" she said with a smile.

"It's nice to meet you. My name's Maya and I'm lost."

"But the test is about to start!"

Maya closed her wings around herself again.

"What's wrong?" asked Cleo in a sweet voice. "Are you scared?"

"I'm going to fail! I just know it!"

"I'm sure you are going to do great! And if you don't try, you won't really know, right? Now go through that archway and down the corridor, and you won't be lost anymore."

Maya smiled gratefully and flew off to catch up with the others.

Cleo watched her speed away and wondered what to do with the rest of her disastrous day. She couldn't just hang around the school all day, so she decided to go back to her room and read a good book. Cleo loved to read because she could disappear into a different world. She could be a brave hero fighting pirates, or an explorer of unknown lands.

Clippety-clop!

Cleo turned. The sound of hooves came from somewhere in the distance. "Theodora, is that you?" she called. No one answered. Feeling a little nervous, Cleo crept back into her hiding place behind the door.

Just then, a figure in a blue cloak walked

right past her. Curious, Cleo decided to follow.

They walked for a long time, through corridor after corridor. Finally, they came to a door that led to one of the castle's many gardens. The figure in the blue cloak slipped into the garden, but Cleo paused. She knew she was not allowed in because it was one of the areas used for the Melowies' entrance exam. She looked around and thought about going back to her room. But she could not ignore her curiosity.

"Anybody there?" she asked. She pushed the door open slowly, and when she saw what was on the other side, she gasped.

4
The Entrance Exam

Meanwhile, Maya had caught up with the others without anyone noticing she was missing.

Principal Gia led the Melowies into the assembly hall. It was a beautiful room with a hanging garden in place of one of its walls. The Melowies were looking around in wonder when a shower of tiny crystals began to fall gently from above. The color of the

shining glass ceiling changed from a soft yellow to orange, pink, and red. The colors kept changing and getting brighter and brighter, until the hall was filled with a wonderful rainbow.

"Ooh!" everyone cried at once.

Just then, four beautiful pegasuses

Ms. Decorum

Ms. Magister

appeared on the rainbow and flew together into the center of the room.

"I'd like to introduce you to some of the teachers you will be working with here at the Castle of Destiny," announced Principal Gia. The rainbow faded away as the teachers took their place next to her.

Ms. Mercury

Ms. Bernice

"Meet Ms. Decorum, who teaches etiquette, and Ms. Magister, who teaches math and pegasus science." Ms. Magister gave a little nod and adjusted her glasses, while the principal continued with the introductions. "Ms. Mercury will teach you aerobatics, and Ms. Bernice teaches pegasus literature."

"They all look so strict!" whispered Electra to another student.

"It's time for the most important part of your first day: the entrance exam," continued Gia. "You will be divided into groups of four. When it's your turn, you will go through one of the examination doors, into the garden. There you will have the chance to prove that the Castle of Destiny is the right place for you."

"Oh no . . . ," moaned a little voice next to Cora. She turned to see Maya trying to hide in her own wings.

"Are you okay?" Cora asked.

"It's just that . . . I'm afraid I won't pass the test," Maya whispered.

"Come on! You'll be fine!" Electra interrupted, nudging Cora aside.

Cora snorted and tried to ignore her.

"I think I'll wait in the back so I can go last," Maya said as the others began to form an orderly line.

"I don't think so," cried Electra. "Come with me!"

"Let her do what she wants!" snorted Selena.

"Would you let me through, please?" snapped Cora, who hated not being first.

A firm voice interrupted the squabble. "You four! What are you doing there?" asked Principal Gia. She didn't wait for an answer. "If you are so eager for attention, perhaps the four of you should go first."

5
In the Maze

The four Melowies followed the principal into the garden. Four examination doors surrounded a square of thick, tall bushes. The doors were glittering magical barriers that shone like mirrors and hid the castle's magical secrets.

"Wings out, chin up, look proud," Cora muttered as she walked calmly through one of the doors. The gate shook and changed color like a soap bubble, and then the filly disappeared.

The other three Melowies gasped.

"Come along, now," instructed Principal Gia. "You, girls, too."

Maya, Electra, and Selena went to stand in front of the other doors.

"Okay, here we go," Maya whispered to herself, trying not to tremble. She took a deep breath and walked through the rainbow doorway. "Wow!" she cried a

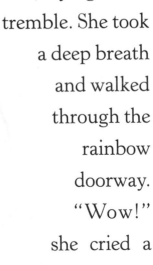

moment later. Maya was standing at the entrance to a garden maze made up of leaves in every imaginable shade of green. She timidly stepped into the leafy web. The branches formed an emerald roof over her head. "I guess you really can't fly out of this one," she said, growing more and more nervous.

As she made her way through the twists and turns of the maze, the pathways grew more narrow, and the tangle of branches and leaves got thicker. Maya stopped in front of a high hedge with a path running through it that was so narrow, it was more like a hole. She plucked up her courage and peeked inside. She couldn't see anything! The hole was pitch-black, and Maya was afraid of the dark!

She forced herself to concentrate even though she was trembling in fear. Had she chosen the wrong path? Maybe she should return to the beginning and start over. But when she turned around, a vine wrapped itself around her ankle. "Hey!" she cried, trying to pull away. The harder she tugged, more vines slithered out from the hedges and tried to grab her.

Maya looked around in a panic. Using magic without permission was forbidden at the Castle of Destiny. She would definitely fail the entrance exam if she did that. Going back was impossible, but if she stayed here, she would end up a prisoner of the vines. The only way out was through the hole in the hedge! Maya took a deep breath, shut her eyes, and went in.

She stumbled around in the dark, trying to find her way. Branches scratched her neck and face, but she kept moving forward, and even managed to open her eyes.

But the moment she did, she saw something that made her scream in fright! A pair of eyes stared back at her.

"Aaah!"

A young pegasus with bits of twigs and leaves caught in her coat stood in front of Maya.

"Wait, please don't run away!" cried the little pegasus. "It's me, Cleo. We met in the castle earlier, remember? I came in here by mistake. I have to get out of here before Principal Gia finds out, or I will be in big trouble!"

"Get out of here?" repeated Maya as soon as she was over her fright.

"Yes, but I can't find my way back," explained Cleo. "I'm not a Melowy, you know. I can't take this test the way you girls can. How did you get in here?"

"From over there," said Maya, pointing to the hole in the high hedge.

"Thanks." Cleo smiled. She was about to go, but Maya stopped her.

"Cleo, do you think you could you stay with me?"

Cleo bit her lip thoughtfully. "I don't

know if I can. I could get into so much trouble with Principal Gia."

"Oh, pretty please!" Maya begged. "I promise that I'll do everything I have to do to pass the test myself. But could you stay with me, please? I don't want to be alone."

Cleo thought for a moment and nodded. She couldn't leave the poor filly alone and scared. Side by side, she and Maya headed off to find their way through the maze.

6
A Flower Made of Wings

Not long after, Maya and Cleo came upon a big hole in the ground. Careful not to fall in, they leaned over it and looked down. The pit was deep, even bottomless, and icy-cold air rose up from the darkness. Far, far below they could see a golden light.

Maya shivered and held on to Cleo. The two pegasuses looked around, trying to find another way out of the maze. The roof of branches and leaves was gone, but there was a huge glass dome in its place.

When they looked down again, Maya and Cleo discovered that they weren't alone. Standing around the top of the pit, and at the end of paths that looked a lot like the one they'd just come from, were Selena, Cora, and Electra.

"I had to crawl through a tunnel full of thorny plants!" Selena yelled over the howling wind that was coming from the pit.

"I got lost in a forest!" cried Electra. "The trees were so thick that there was barely any sunlight!"

"What about you, Cora?" asked Electra.

Cora was about to answer when she noticed Maya and Cleo across the pit. She stared coldly into Cleo's eyes. "You're the one who got tangled up in the flag," she said.

"That's me," nodded Cleo.

Electra introduced herself "Hi, I'm Electra, from the Day Realm. Miss Icicles here is from the Winter Realm, and the one who doesn't speak very much is Selena, from the Night Realm. The chicken next to you is Maya. But I guess you already know that because you came with her. She comes

from the Spring Realm. Which realm are you from?"

"Oh, I'm not a Melowy," explained Cleo. "I'm not supposed to be here. I got lost."

"Oh." Electra shrugged. "Well, you might still come in handy. We're in a real mess!"

"But she just said that she's not a Melowy! She can't stay with us!" Cora snorted.

"What does it matter? We'll probably never get out of here anyway," Maya groaned, a worried expression on her face. "There's no going back. I've already tried that. And I don't know about you, but I'll never be brave enough to jump down there."

Electra nodded and said, "I tried to, but watch this . . ." She stepped into the pit, but instead of falling, she floated. The powerful wind kept her from sinking. She just hovered there in the icy gusts before struggling back to solid ground.

One by one, all the Melowies tried it, and the same thing happened. The wind ruffled their manes, but none of them fell as much as an inch. Flapping their wings didn't even help.

Electra tried getting a running start and jumping straight down, but only ended up colliding with Selena.

"Oww!" groaned Selena, rubbing her sore head.

A smile spread across Cleo's face. "Didn't you see what happened?" she asked in excitement.

Maya nodded, her eyes widening. "For just a moment, you were falling!"

"Maybe the weight of one pegasus isn't enough," suggested Cleo. "Maybe if we all hold on to one another, we'll be heavy enough to fall to the bottom."

"See, Cora!" cried Electra with a wink. "Cleo might not be a Melowy, but she is useful!"

"On the count of three, we all jump and try to stay together," said Cleo, wrapping a wing around Maya's back. "Ready?"

Cora, Selena, Maya, and Electra all nodded. Maybe working together was the solution!

"One . . . two . . . *three!*" shouted Cleo as she jumped into the pit, pulling Maya after her—just in case.

"*Whee!*" screamed Electra, grabbing hold of Cora's wing.

Cora rolled her eyes. *That silly girl is ruining a serious moment,* she thought. But she had no time to complain because it looked like Cleo's plan was working. Selena grabbed hold of her left wing. Maya wrapped a wing over Cleo, who'd wrapped a wing around Electra.

All five pegasuses had soon formed a tight circle. Slowly but surely, they started drifting downward, floating on the wind like a flower, a giant dandelion in the breeze. Without letting go of one another, they got closer and closer to the golden light at the bottom of the pit.

But there was no time to celebrate. Suddenly, everything around them changed!

7

A Surprise Student

The Melowies drifted through a golden pool of light and found themselves in a room lit by a thousand candles that danced in the silence. Principal Gia appeared from the shadows with two of the school's teachers.

"Congratulations!" she announced. "You are the first group to pass the test."

Cleo looked around in amazement. She had lived at the Castle of Destiny since she was tiny, but she'd never seen this room before. She stared at a realistic model of the castle with a lifelike sea of clouds all around it that sat in one corner of the room. But Cleo was too worried to be amazed.

"Well done, all of you!" said Principal Gia. "Even though you are all very different, you were able to work together as a team."

Cora, Selena, Electra, and Maya all smiled proudly. But Cleo grew more and more uncomfortable with every passing second. She knew she shouldn't be there!

"I'm so sorry, Principal Gia! I didn't mean to sneak through the examination door!" Cleo said all in one breath when she'd found the courage to speak. "I promise it won't happen again!" Cleo hung her head and started to walk away.

"Cleo, step forward, please." The principal gave her a serious look.

Cleo gulped and did as Gia had ordered. But Maya immediately stepped up to join her.

"Principal Gia . . . ," the shy Melowy began in a whisper. "Please don't punish Cleo! She didn't mean to make trouble. And she was a huge help! We never would have gotten through the maze without her."

"It's true!" Electra joined in. "Cleo was wonderful!"

"Yes!" Selena nodded.

Cora was silent for a moment, but then said, "Cleo acted like a true Melowy."

Cleo was so surprised that she almost didn't hear Principal Gia start speaking again.

"Calm down! I don't plan to punish her. Anyone who passes the test has what it takes to attend school at the Castle of Destiny. Cleo, even though you don't have a symbol on your wings, we are ready to welcome you as a new student. I'm sure you'll do very well."

Cleo couldn't believe it. She was going to be a student at the Castle of Destiny, just like the Melowies!

Once the test was complete, the girls were led to their new rooms in the Butterfly Tower.

"Me first, me first!" Electra shouted, pushing her way through the door. "Hey! My case is here already!"

At the Castle of Destiny, every Melowy brought a case full of memories from home to decorate the wall behind her bed. Some Melowies, like Electra, started packing their cases when they were very young, dreaming of their first day at the school. The rest of the group trotted in after her. Even Cleo was excited to settle into her new room.

"Where should I put these, my little cupcake?" asked Theodora, who burst into the room carrying a stack of Cleo's books.

Cleo smiled. She might not have a case of memories for her wall, but she did have something special of her own: her favorite books.

"Just over there, please, Theodora. I'll sort them out later."

The cook looked at her with tears in her eyes. Before Cleo could escape, Theodora gave her a great big hug. "My little girl is growing up!"

"Theodora!" Cleo felt a little embarrassed but still enjoyed the warm hug and the smell of chocolate and cinnamon on Theodora's mane.

"I'm so proud of you, my little cream cake! It's going to be hard to see you go!"

"I won't be very far away." Cleo laughed. "I'll be right here inside the castle!" But she knew that Theodora was right. Cleo was starting a whole new life!

Theodora pinched Cleo's cheek. "I have to go now. I have some work to do in the kitchen," she said as she trotted off.

"Hey, Cleo!" cried Maya after the cook had left. "Look, your case is here!"

"My what?" said Cleo in amazement. There, sitting next to her bed was a bright blue valise. *There must be some mistake,* thought Cleo. The case probably belonged to another student. It had to have been brought here by accident.

Just to be sure, Cleo opened it. Inside she found something that warmed her heart. "My blanket!" she exclaimed, and buried her cheek into the soft orange fabric that she had been wrapped in when she was left on the front steps of the Castle of Destiny. "And my stuffed pegasus.

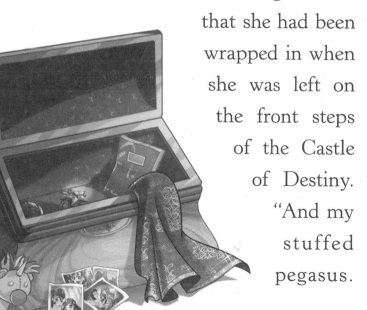

You're squished, you poor thing! And my first writing book. And photos of me and Theodora!"

The case was almost empty, but Cleo noticed something shiny down at the bottom. She picked up the mysterious object. It was a necklace with a star-shaped pendant that seemed strangely familiar to Cleo even though she'd never seen it before.

"It looks like a locket," said Selena when Cleo showed it to the others.

The pendant was a glittering blue stone with a small oval shape in the center. Cleo tried to open it, but nothing happened. She put the necklace on and it made her feel happy, as if it were some kind of precious amulet.

"So who packed the case for you?" asked Cora.

"I think it must be my arrival day present," answered Cleo with a smile.

"Arrival day?" asked Maya in surprise.

"Yes, the anniversary of when I arrived here. Principal Gia found me on the front steps of the castle when I was a baby," said Cleo, heading for the door. "Every year since, we've had a party to celebrate. But I'll tell you all about it later. There's something I have to do!"

8
Arrival Day Party

Principal Gia sat behind an imposing crystal desk in her office on the top floor of the keep, talking to Theodora. "The maze for our test is planned so that the students find one another just before they come to the biggest challenge," Principal Gia was saying. "They can only pass the test if they work together. I wasn't expecting this."

"Has a pegasus who was not a Melowy

ever passed the exam before?" asked Theodora.

"Not in many years," the principal said. "It hasn't happened since—"

"Gia! Gia!" cried Cleo, trotting into the office. Theodora slammed the drawer of the crystal desk shut. Cleo thought she looked strangely embarrassed. But she had more important things on her mind. "Tell me the truth, Gia! You made sure I took the Melowy test and packed my memory case of memories!"

"The case was a gift from me, yes," the principal said with a smile. "But I had nothing to do with your taking the test. I see you are wearing the pendant. It looks lovely on you."

"Did it belong to my mother?" asked Cleo.

"It might have. Unfortunately, as you know, I never met her. But this pendant was with you when I found you," said Principal Gia, growing serious. "Now you're old enough to care for it."

"It looks like it opens, but I can't seem to make it work."

"Things don't always work the way we want them to, hmm? Perhaps it will only open when it's ready to open. Or when you are ready to see what's inside. Happy arrival day, Cleo!"

Cleo looked at Theodora and asked, "You weren't hiding something from me when I came in, were you?"

Theodora coughed. "Um, sugar pie, where do you get these ideas from? You've always had far too much imagination!"

Cleo was sure she had noticed a piece of blue cloth hanging out of the drawer that Theodora had rushed to close. It looked just like the cloak worn by the stranger who'd guided her to the examination door. But Cleo didn't push the issue. She just smiled and ran off.

*   *   *

When Cleo got back to her room, there was a surprise waiting.

"Happy arrival day, Cleo!" cried Maya.

While Cleo had been away, her roommate had gone to the kitchen and gotten permission to make an arrival-day chocolate-cream cake. "I couldn't find any candles, though," said Maya. "And someone used up all the frosting. Sorry."

Cleo was touched. "Thank you so much, Maya! The cake is wonderful, and so are you!"

"It was the least I could do, after what you did for me in the maze," Maya answered with a blush. "I don't know if I would have been brave enough to finish the test without you."

Just then, Selena came into the room and gave Cleo a smile. "Happy arrival day!"

"Thank you," Cleo said, looking around. "I like how you've decorated your part of the room. It's so cool!"

Selena grinned. "Thank you! If you like, I could help you decorate your wall."

"*Cake! Cake! Cake!*" Electra came in next, squealing. "Finally! Maya wouldn't even let me lick the spoon! Wait until you see what I've got for you! Are you ready to party?"

Electra reached into her messy case and pulled out some speakers. She turned them on, and soon the room filled with wild music.

"What's all this noise?" asked Cora, rushing into the room.

"Hey, Cora, chill out," said Electra.

Cora looked her up and down. Then, surprisingly, she did a perfect pirouette. She smiled and said, "Let's dance!"

Everyone joined in, and soon they were giggling like old friends. Each of the girls was so happy to be there. And so ready to discover what her future had in store.

Meanwhile in the Night Realm, four pega-suses stood around a darkened room and exchanged grim looks in the trembling candlelight.

"Your Immensity, the new Melowies have arrived at Destiny," said a low voice. "With them, there's—"

"It changes nothing," interrupted the Queen of the Night. A crown of dark stones glittered on her head. "Nothing can distract us from our goal," she added. "Our time is coming. We will seize the Castle of Destiny and Aura will be ours . . ."

Read on for a sneak peek of the next
exciting moment in the Melowies' journey:

The Song
of the Moon

A Surprise for the Melowies

The Castle of Destiny changed at the beginning of every school year. The castle's silent corridors, high ceilings, and steep spiral staircases filled with laughter and friendship. The castle turned into a place where promising young Melowies came to search for their own destinies.

"Hey, girls! The first week of school is finally over!" cried Electra. She ran out of the science lab like a cyclone of red curls.

"When do we start lessons in the Art of Powers? I can't wait to learn how to use mine! In the Day Realm, Melowies make beams of light! I wouldn't even know where to start."

"Not yet," said Cora, throwing cold water on Electra's enthusiasm. "First we have to take our core lessons, which will be hard. I almost fell asleep in pegasus science today!"

"Me, too!" Electra said. "But that's because I was too excited to sleep last night! Just think! We survived our first week at the Castle of Destiny! We made it!" She found a gap in the crowded corridor and skipped away.

Cora shook her head. "No one behaves like that in the Winter Realm."

"Come on, Cora!" teased Cleo with a chuckle. "Do you always have to be Miss Icicles?"

Selena was so deep in her own thoughts that she passed right by her two friends. Maya, though, was still dragging her hooves. "Is something wrong?" asked Cleo.

"It's true. We have made it," whispered the pink filly. "But what if I'm not up to it? They have already given us a mountain of homework to do. I still haven't finished the geology project, and now we've got two chapters of science to finish by tomorrow!"

Cleo just smiled. "Come on, Maya! You're doing just fine. Even Ms. Pangea said so when you answered that question about the Spring Realm!"

Maya blushed. "Well, that was easy! That's where I'm from! But you got a ten on the first literature assignment. I don't know how you did it."

"I think it's because I really like reading."

"And you were fantastic at the first aerobatics lesson."

"Oh, that's only because I have been secretly watching flying lessons since I was little!" Cleo said.

Cleo was the only Melowy who didn't know which of the four realms she came from. She grew up at the Castle of Destiny after the school principal found her on the front steps when she was just a baby. She'd never been allowed to mix with the students who lived in the castle, until this year. The day of the entrance exam she discovered that she was a Melowy as well. All at once, her dreams had come true. Best of all, she made four new friends, each from a different realm.

EXPLORE DESTINY WITH THE MELOWIES AS THEY DISCOVER THEIR MAGICAL POWERS!

Hidden somewhere beyond the highest clouds is the Castle of Destiny, a school for very special students. They're the Melowies, young pegasuses born with a symbol on their wings and a hidden magical power. And the time destined for them to meet has now arrived.